This edition published by Parragon Books Ltd in 2014
and distributed by

Parragon Inc.
440 Park Avenue South, 13th Floor
New York, NY 10016
www.parragon.com

Copyright © Parragon Books Ltd 2014

Written by Frances Prior-Reeves
Designed by Talking Design
Illustrations by Carol Seatory

ISBN 978-1-4723-4050-4

Printed in China

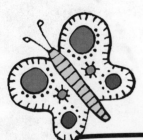

Dream Big, Draw Bigger

PaRragon

Bath · New York · Cologne · Melbourne · Delhi
Hong Kong · Shenzhen · Singapore · Amsterdam

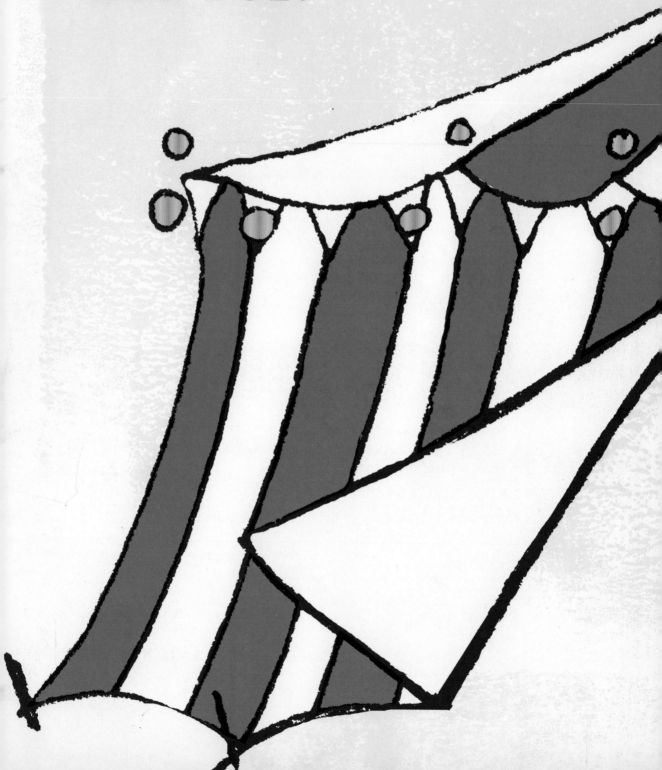

Draw the inside of this

BIG TOP.

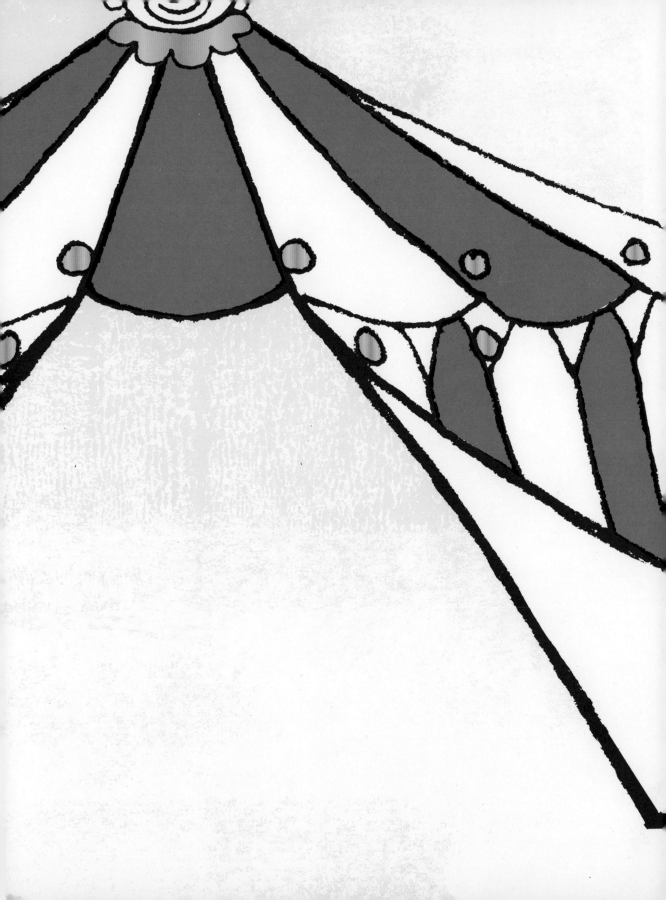

Draw something

massive!

**Draw
something**
minuscule.

SPACE FOR
YOU TO DRAW
ANYTHING.

Make these pages into a MAZE.

Fill these vases with

flowers.

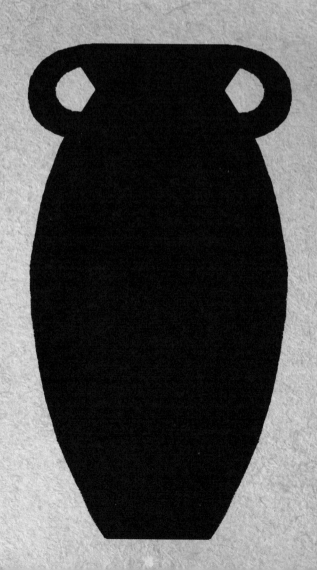

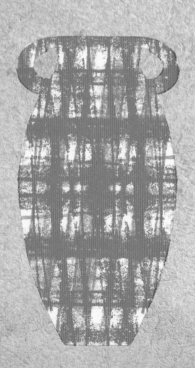

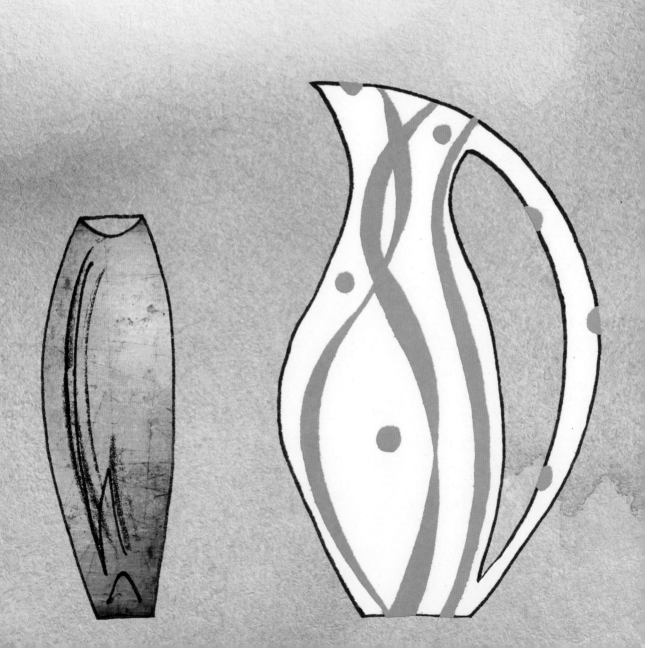

Fill this page with
SQUARES.

Can you transform those squares into clouds?

Fill these craft jars

with safety pins, thread, buttons, and other odds and ends.

Draw an ASTRONAUT
floating in outer space.

Draw the rest of this

elephant.

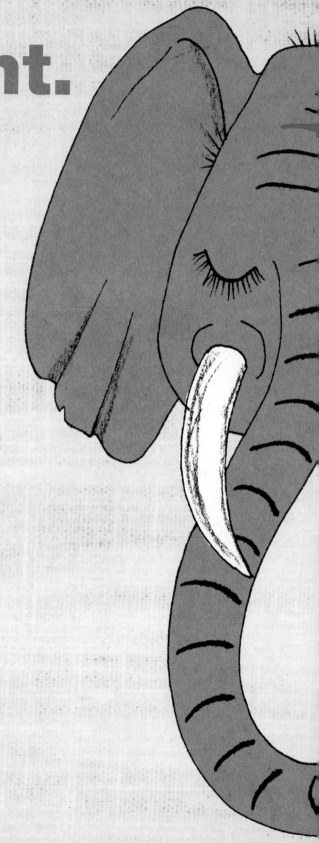

BE PLAYFUL
WHEN YOU
DRAW.

Design this couch.

Add some pillows to it, too.

Color this **pattern.**

Draw ...
a president,
a baseball player,
and a clown.

Now draw one image of all three.

Draw a HORSE
pulling this carriage.

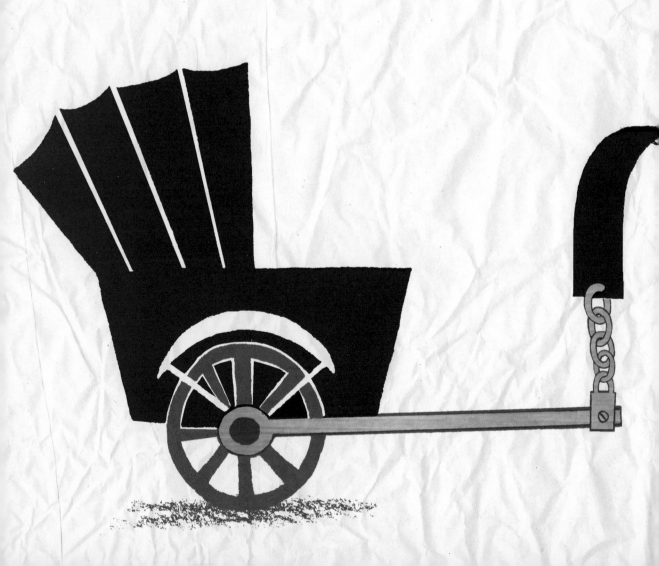

Design your own

money.

Give these feet a

pedicure.

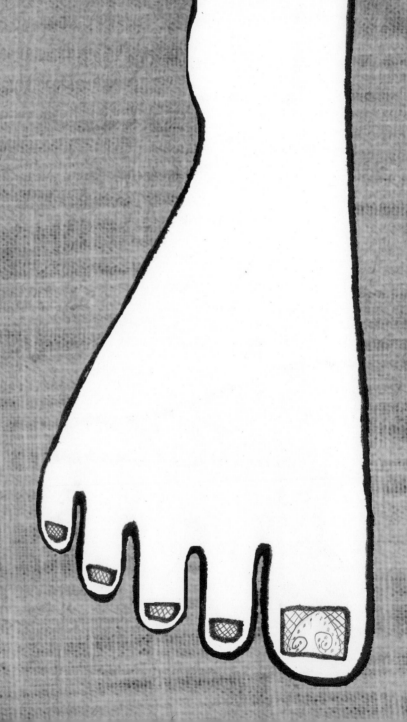

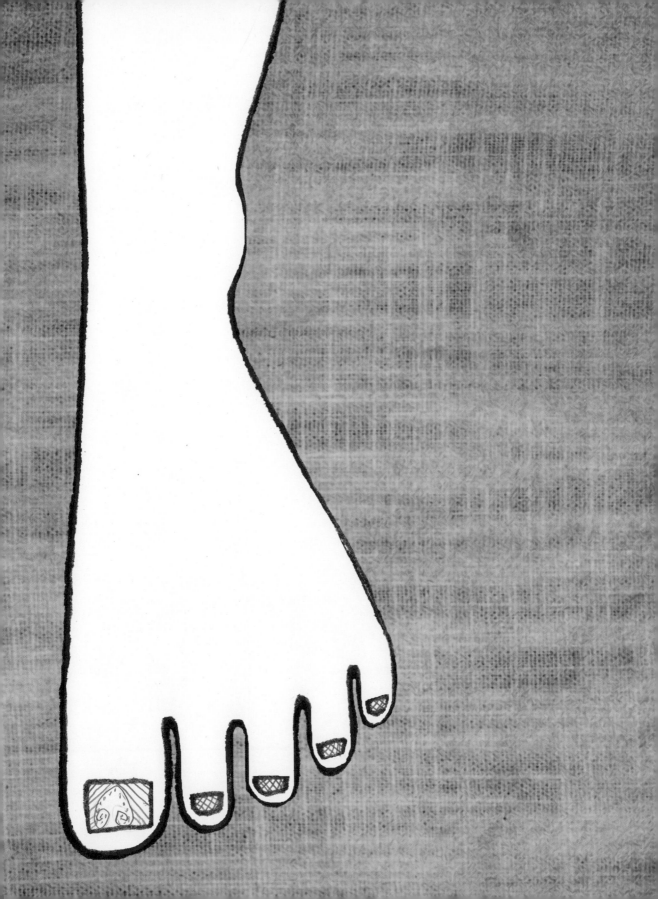

Fill this desert with life.

Draw a troupe of

fire – breathing reptiles .

Draw a self-portrait.

Draw yourself as a ZOMBIE.

Add your
favorite
toppings
to this pizza.

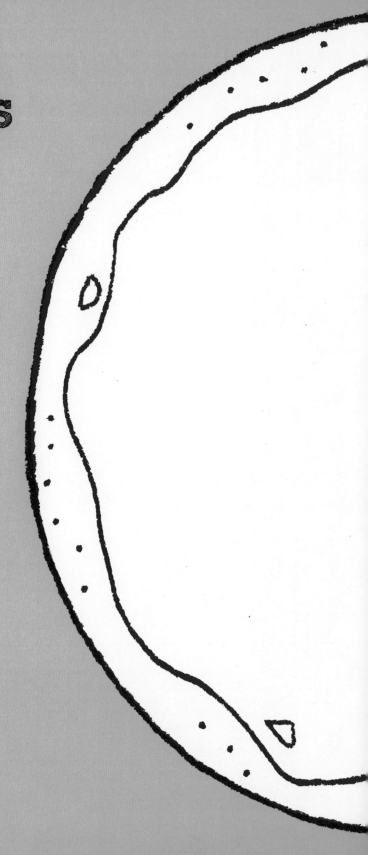

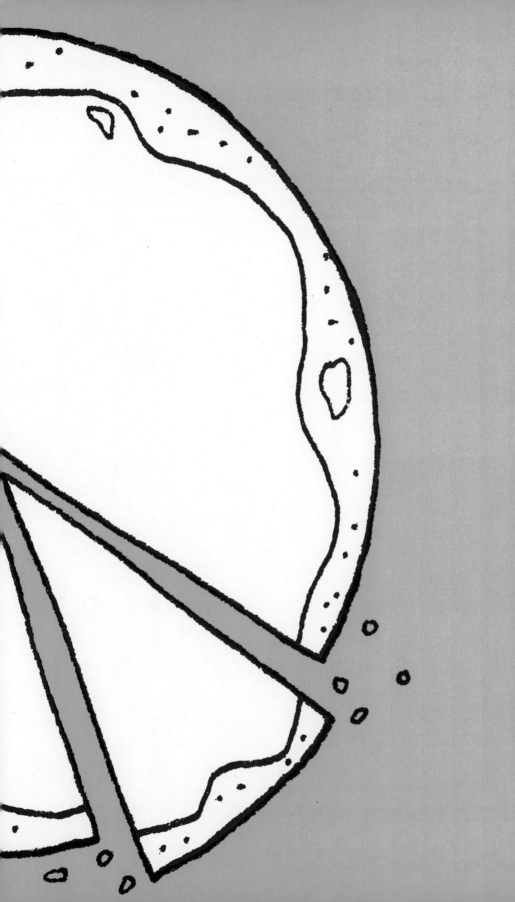

Add some **art** to this gallery.

Draw things that can
float on this lake.

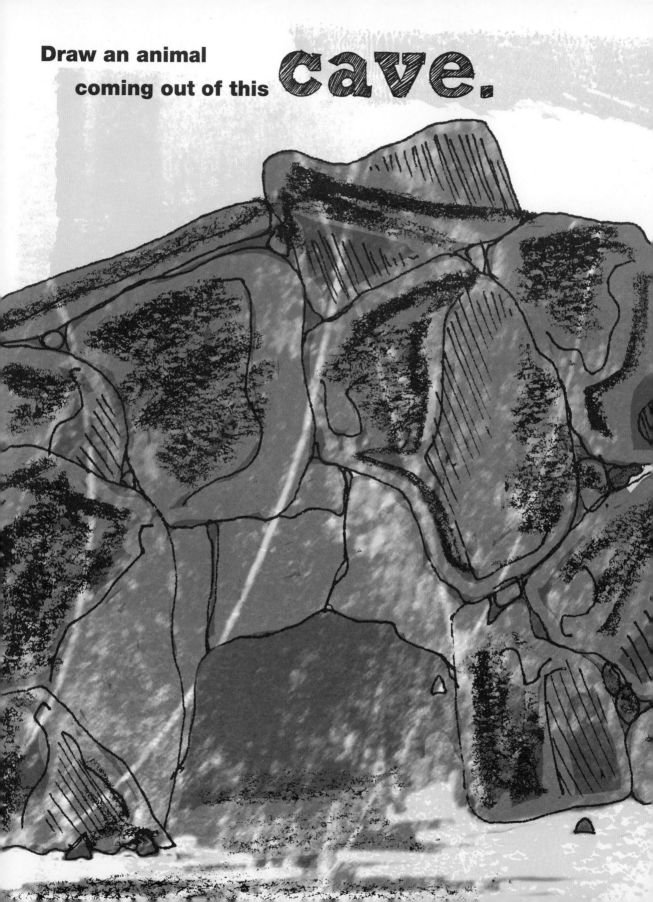

Draw an animal coming out of this cave.

Finish drawing this

castle.

Fill this page with circles.

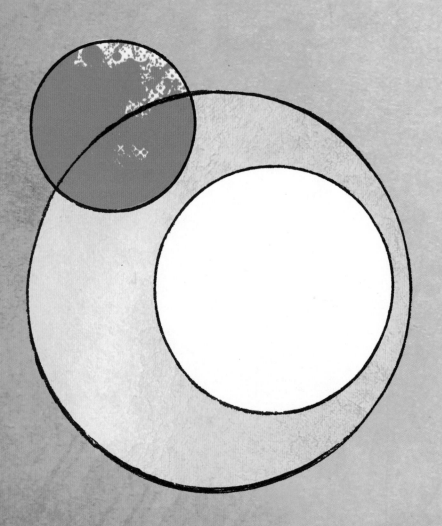

Can you transform those circles into

FLYING OBJECTS?

Draw the
passengers
on this bus.

GRAFFITI
THESE PAGES.

Fill these pages with
COLORFUL STRIPES
to make your own pattern.

Draw
TRASH OVERFLOWING
into a landfill.

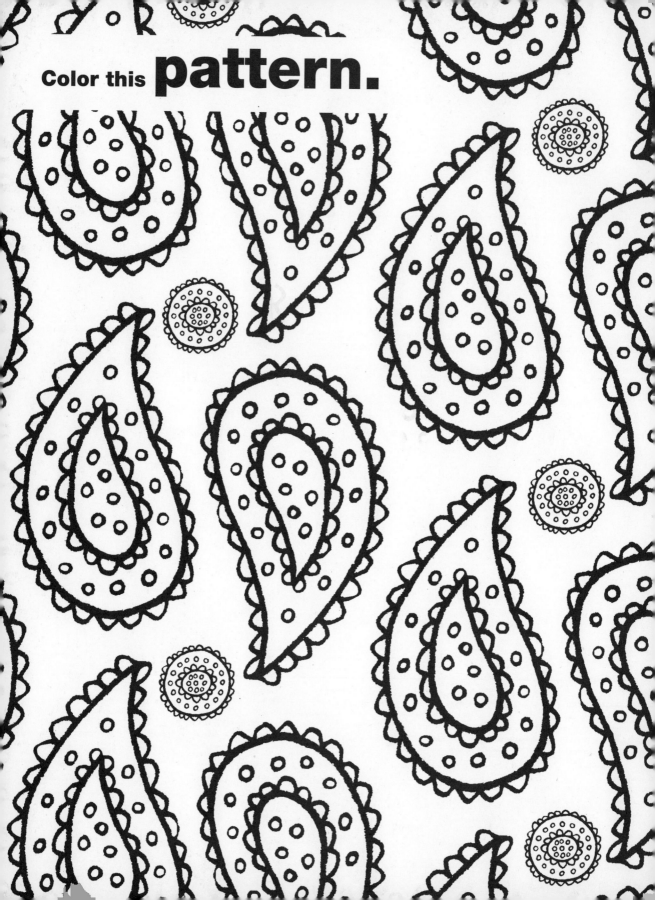

Color this pattern.

Fill this skyline with

balloons.

Draw your favorite

AMUSEMENT PARK RIDES.

IMAGINE,
THEN DRAW.

Draw loot spilling from this

treasure chest.

Draw a
cat swimming ...

... and a
bird jogging.

Add a train to these
RAILROAD TRACKS.

Draw **half of your face** on one side of the circle ...

... and draw half of a **MONSTER'S FACE** on the other.

Draw your favorite animal.

Draw your least favorite animal.

Design a
BEDSPREAD
for this bed.

Draw what's
CREEPING
around in the dark.

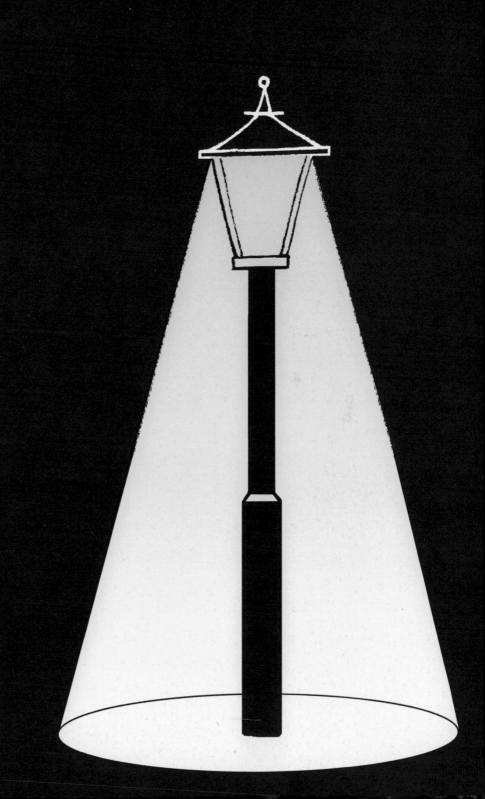

WRAP UP

this boy and girl up for winter.

It's snowing, do they need coats, hats, scarfs, and gloves?

Draw animals
and their offspring.

cat/kitten

dog/puppy

bird/chick

horse/foal

frog/tadpole

kangaroo/joey

cow/calf

WITH DICE.

Add *wings* to this butterfly.

Fill this page with

HEXAGONS.

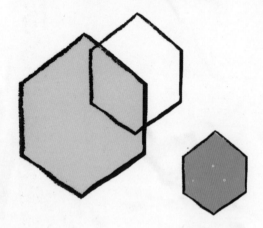

**Give each hexagon an individual
design on this patchwork quilt.**

Draw ...

a tiger,

a raccoon,

and an eagle.

**Now draw one
image of all three.**

Turn these
shapes into faces
and give them each a different emotion.

scared

HAPPY

crying

laughing

longing

Fill these pages with a

BUSY CROWD
of people.

Draw your

FAVORITE DISH

coming out of this oven.

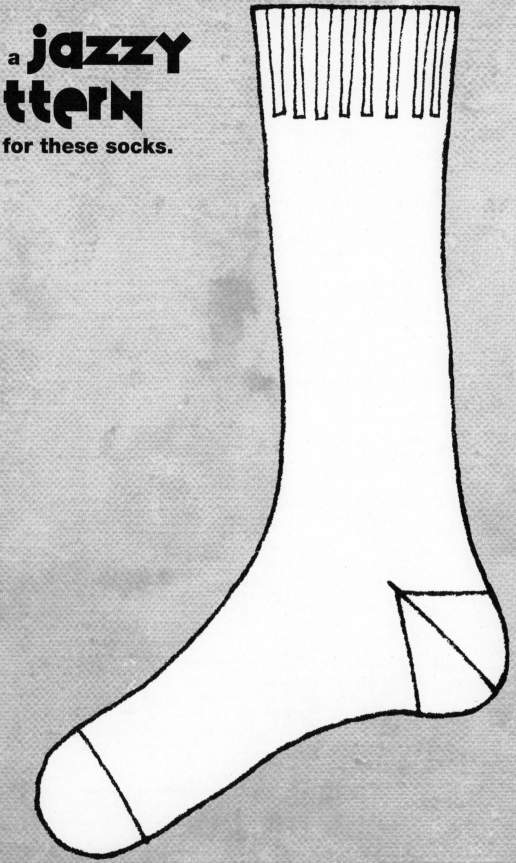

Design a **jazzy pattern** for these socks.

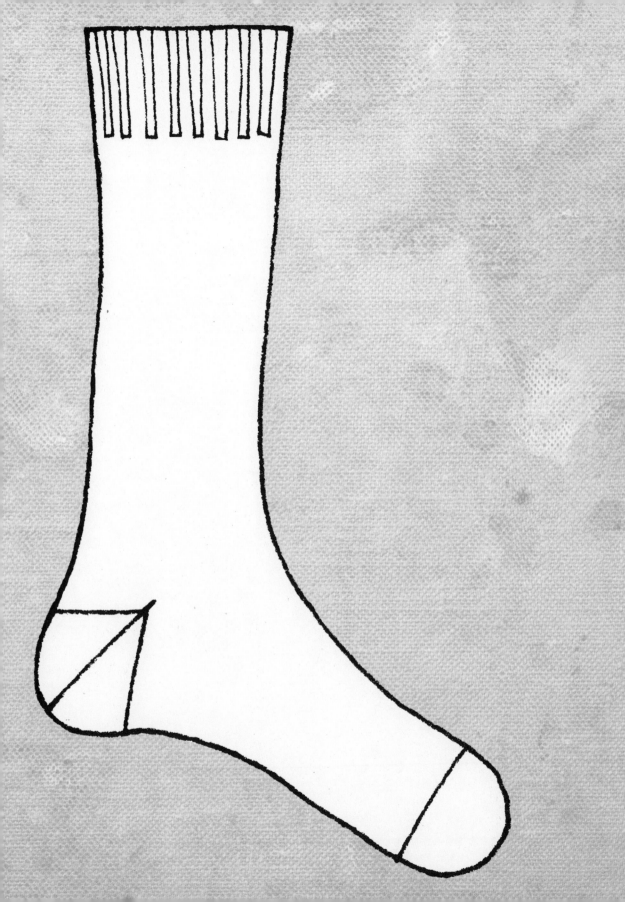

Add someone to this
zip line.

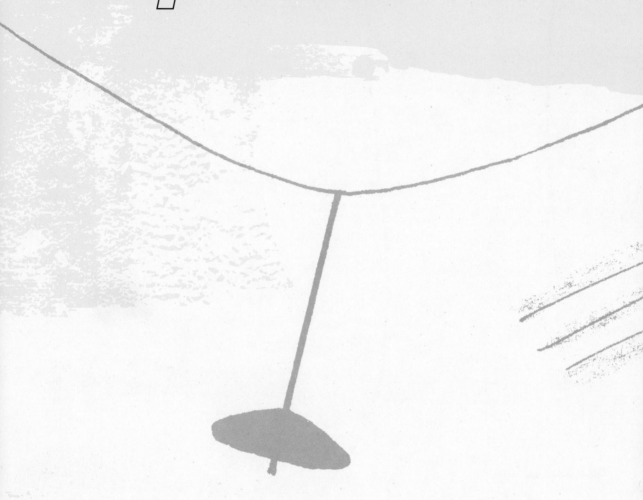

Draw someone
BALANCING
on this tightrope.

Draw a
tall penguin.

Draw a short giraffe.

Can you turn this graph paper into a
polka-dot pattern?

Add some frosting

to these cupcakes.

IDEAS.

Add
SKATEBOARDERS
to this skate ramp.

Add some
pinwheels to the dark.

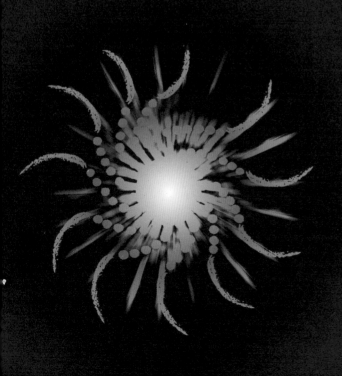

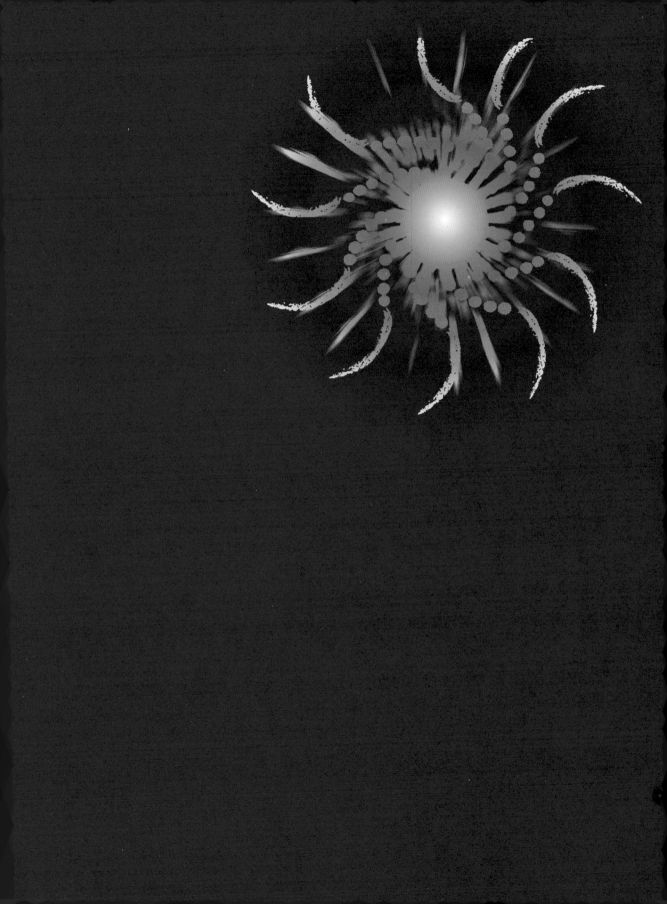

Create a pattern using
four colors.

Fill this page with

Can you transform those hearts into a picture of something you love?

Add bright and colorful designs to these

HAWAIIAN SHIRTS.

Draw things that have sunk to the
bottom of the ocean.

Fill these jars with your
FAVORITE CANDY.

Draw a
FIREFIGHTER
holding this hose.

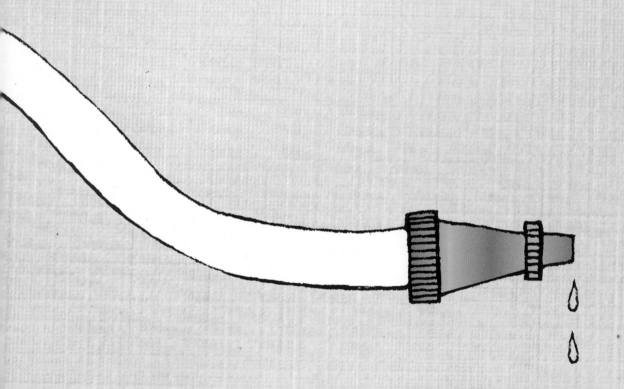

Draw what is on FIRE.

Use as many colors as you can to create an INTRICATE PATTERN.

Add some hats and coats to this

hatstand.

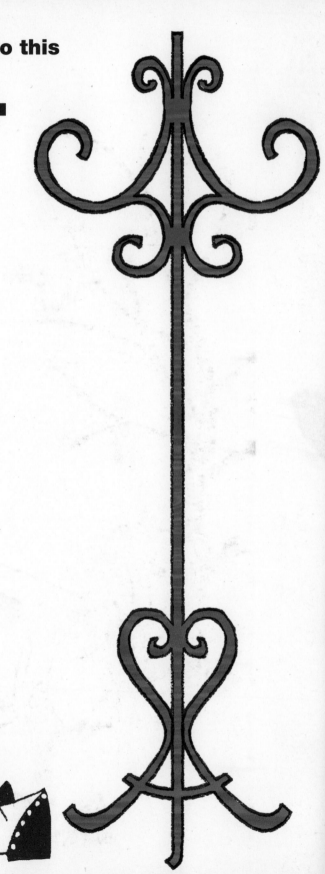